The Christmas Present

Alexander McCabe

Based on the original edition of *The Christmas Present* by Alexander McCabe, first published 2015.

Second edition, July 2016.

Third edition, August 2017.

Alexander McCabe asserts his rights as the publisher of this work.

Illustrations by Fabiana Farcas – www.fiverr.com/fabiuscafarcas

Printed and bound in China.

www.gabrieltheelf.com

ISBN: 978-1-912435-00-5

FOR GABRIEL

Not yet old enough to understand the wondrous joys of Christmas, but when he does, I hope it never leaves him.

For his elf's sake...

ACKNOWLEDGMENTS

To my son, Gabriel, who inspired this tale and owns my heart.

To my wife, Marie, who believes in – and understands – my imaginative madness.

To the children of Keiss Primary School and their head teacher, and my friend, Katy Laidlaw.
Thank you so much for reading and reviewing my book. A special thanks for the pictures you all drew
too! The reviews were brutally honest, heartwarming, and hilarious.

Finally, thank you so much for reading, and may I take this opportunity to wish you and your family
a very Merry Christmas and – as we say in Scotland – may the coming year bring
health, wealth, and happiness.

CHAPTERS

THE GREAT ESCAPE

I hate you!

The front door was the only escape from both my mum and yet another pathetic Christmas that she had planned for just the two of us. As I ran down the path and out into the street, every window I passed had a beautiful tree that held sparkling fairy lights and shiny tinsel wrapped all around it. Small chocolate Santas seemed to be hanging heavily from each branch. I could only imagine all of the wonderful presents that were under each of those trees.

That only made me madder.

The tears burned my eyes but they were cold by the time they reached my cheeks. I kept running, faster and faster. I wanted to be far away from here. Far away from my mum. Far away from our house. Far away from all these bright and shiny windows and

all their happy and joyful trees.

I hate it.

I hate it all.

You can keep your Christmas! I'm almost ten. I know that there is no Santa Claus. I know better than all these other kids in my class and in my school who still believe in him. If he was real – Santa Claus – he would have given me better presents. Bigger presents. More expensive presents. I wouldn't need to be making paper chains with pieces of coloured card, glitter, and glue with my mum. No, the real Santa Claus would make sure we had tinsel, and fairy lights, and chocolates hanging from every branch of *our* tree.

I was the unluckiest kid in the world, the only one who didn't have any of these things.

It was only then that I realised that I was no longer running. I was standing right under the very last streetlight at the very edge of our village. Through the light snow that was slowly falling all around me, and a whole five miles away in the distance, I could see the town where my dad lived with his new family. This streetlight was my boundary. My mum had made it very clear that I wasn't allowed to go beyond this point.

Ever.

Well, tonight was different. She didn't matter anymore. I was going to find my dad and live with him and his new family. His new family had everything I could ever want. They would have a great Christmas with a nice tree, fantastic presents, and a big turkey dinner with all the trimmings.

We would have chicken. Again.

I don't actually like turkey and I don't even know what 'the trimmings' are, but I'm pretty sure that I don't like them either. Not that any of that really matters. Slowly and deliberately I walked beyond the lamppost, carefully looking all around to see if anyone was watching me. Only when I was certain nobody could see me, I took a brave step beyond the circle of light that was spread all over the fresh snow that covered the pavement and the road – into the darkness. I wasn't scared. Not really. I quickly jumped back under the light and looked back down the street in the direction of my house.

And my mum.

Unusually, the village seemed to be deserted. Well, except for the army of snowmen who were lazily standing guard in every garden that I could see. I knew they wouldn't and, more importantly, couldn't tell on me. This was my chance. There was nobody else watching and so there was nobody who could tell my mum that they had seen me leaving. By the time she realised, I'd be with my dad.

His new family would be my new family too.

The happy thought pushed me back into the darkness and the bright lights of the town pulled me towards them. I walked slowly on my tiptoes as, with each new step, I expected to feel my mum's hand on my collar pulling me back into the village. After

what felt like forever – it must have been at least five minutes – there was still nobody around, I began to relax and walk normally. There, in the distance, like a big cake with the most beautiful candles on top, I could see the town.

My dad's town.

My new town.

My new home.

The snow crunched under my feet and the cold started to come through my sneakers. I should have worn my shoes. Not to worry, Dad will buy me a new pair when I see him. He buys my school shoes every year. In fact, I was due a new pair anyway. The shoes he had bought me in the summer had been too big for me and I hated them. *'Good school shoes that you can grow into'* was what my mum had said when we bought them, but now they were too tight. Anyway, the sneakers would just make the journey quicker.

I'll be at Dad's in no time.

It was then that I saw the lights. Two individual beams dancing in the distance but coming straight towards me. Whoever it was, they were heading into the village and they would definitely know my mum. Everybody in the village knows my mum. If they saw me, they would stop and take me back. I couldn't go back. I didn't want to go back.

I knew then that the simplest solution was not to be caught.

However, that was easier said than done. There was no time to hide in the fields and, anyway, they would see me there. At this time of year, the fields were flat and covered in snow. Staring directly at the car, I could see that it was fast coming towards me. Just ahead, on my left, there was a high hedgerow and, behind it, there was a small forest. Well, maybe not an actual forest, but there were enough trees to make it scary.

It was certainly scary to me.

Especially now.

At night.

Yet there was no choice. If they caught me, they would see that I've been crying. I'm almost ten. I'm far too old to be crying. Crying is for babies. I need to be a big boy, and big boys aren't afraid of anything.

At least that's what my dad told me.

Well, that's what he told me a while ago. Maybe two or three visits ago. He keeps promising to see me each week but, then, something always seems to come up. It upsets my mum but I understand. He has a big important job to do and that keeps him very busy, but it's great when he can make it. We do talk on the phone though, when he always asks if I've been a good boy. I always say yes even when there are times that it isn't quite true.

Mum never tells him any different.

Today I haven't quite been good, but I can be brave and be a big boy. He will understand when I tell him. It won't be long now, and quicker still if I manage to avoid being caught by whoever is in the car heading towards the village.

Heading towards my mum.

I run as fast as my sneakers can carry me over the snow to where there is a small gap in the hedge that welcomes me into the forest. Crouching down, the twigs and branches hide me from any unwanted attention, but also gives me the perfect view of the road. As the car gets closer, a scary thought races into my head.

I hope it's not my dad's car!

2

THE FOREST

The car seemed to slow as it got close to me and all I could do was hold my breath and tightly close my eyes as I listened to it crawl passed me. It was only when I couldn't hear it anymore that I dared to open my eyes. Well, actually, it was only one eye. I kept my left eye firmly closed and peeked through my right. Making sure there was nobody else on the road, I let out my breath and watched it disappear through the hedge and follow the direction of the car back to the village. As I went to step back through the gap and back onto the road – away from the scary forest that I had absolutely refused to look into – I heard a twig snap.

Behind me.

I froze and was instantly terrified. Whatever it was, if I couldn't see them, they couldn't see me. Isn't that what my mum had always said when I told her there were monsters under my bed? Only, this wasn't my bed. At that moment, I suddenly wished I was in my bed. At least there I'd be all warm and cosy; safe and secure with Mum ready to fight all the monsters. Those that were real and not so real.

"Shhhh, we don't want to scare him now, do we? That would never do. What would Santa say then? I'd be in so much trouble if we scared him. Even more trouble than I'm already in."

Whoever was talking – actually, they were whispering, but their words were so clear in the silent night that they nearly deafened me – whoever it was, they were very close behind me. Too close. My whole body was perfectly still and both my eyes were now wide open and firmly fixed upon the car's taillights as it disappeared slowly into the distance. It was a few seconds that felt like forever before I found the courage to just jump up and race out through the gap in the hedge and back out onto the empty road. It was only when I'd crossed to the other side did I dare stop running and turn to see if there was anyone following me.

"Are you happy now? You scared him. Santa is going to be so cross with me. He won't be cross with you. Oh no, not you. Of course not you. You, as everybody knows, are one of his favourites. But then, you are everyone's favourite."

"Santa? What are you talking about, Santa? Santa isn't real. *That* is something that *everybody* and *everyone* knows!" I bravely shouted this back into the forest as now I could see where to run – straight towards town. Straight to my dad's house. Whoever they were would have to come out after me. They would never catch me because I can run fast.

Like, really fast. I'm the second fastest boy, and the fourth fastest overall, in my whole class. There are only eleven kids in my whole year – and five of them are girls – but still, I was fast enough to run away from this scary voice in the forest.

Although I had no idea why I wasn't running now.

"Wait…, stop…, where are you going? Come back here at once!" As the voice came out of the forest, I could hear the twigs snapping as something was moving.

Something big.

I don't think I've ever been more afraid. Not even when I was very young and tried to help Mum with decorating the house and I painted the television. She got so mad! Her voice went all weird, but she didn't shout. No, she was very calm as she sent me to my room – '… *and get out of my sight'* is what she said, very calmly – but I knew she was angry. That was as scared as I have ever been.

Well, until now.

Now I really wish I was in my bedroom or running very fast and far away from here. Yet, oddly, all I can do is stand and stare at the gap in the hedge where I had been hiding only a few moments ago. It soon became clear that I was looking in entirely the wrong place.

I shouldn't have been looking *into* the hedge.

I should've been looking *at the top* of the hedge.

"Come back here!" The scary voice cried out from somewhere in the trees.

"I will not and you cannot make me. I shall stay right out here." My voice sounded far braver than I felt.

"I'm not talking to *you*." The voice replied.

"Well, who are you talking to?" This was most peculiar.

"I'm talking to *her*, silly. Now would you come back here? Please!" Another twig snapped or maybe it was a branch breaking. Whatever it was, something was definitely moving around where I'd just been. I peered into the gap, but still couldn't see anything.

"Who is *'her'*, if you don't mind me asking?" Now I was rather more curious than scared.

"I would have thought that was obvious, given that I have already said that she is one of Santa's favourites." The voice didn't sound quite as scary now. It sounded like me when I was being smart with my mum.

I really didn't like it.

"How can it be obvious if Santa isn't real?" My question was already out of my mouth before I could stop it. Mum doesn't like it when that happens. It usually means that I'm in trouble.

Again.

"You take that back! Who says Santa isn't real? Now look what you've done, you've gone and upset her! *Whoa, Gladys, whoa, he didn't mean it, he was only joking…*" As he was speaking, I could hear a little commotion. It was happening right behind the hedge.

Then it happened.

In my curiosity, I hadn't really noticed that I'd been slowly walking back across the road and was now right beside the hedge, still looking into the gap. It was totally black and so I couldn't really see anything, but I could *feel* something. Something's warm breath blew right down my neck.

"AAAAAAAAARRRRRGGGGGHHHHH!"

All at once, I screamed and jumped back into the road, I didn't even have time to look and see if there were any cars coming. Mum would be so upset with me if she knew. Every time we cross the street, she makes sure to tell me, 'Safety first, always look left and right as you go.' Yet, even now that I remembered, I still couldn't check. Although there was a very good reason. A very good reason indeed. One that even Mum would understand.

There, staring at me over the hedge, was…?

No…

Surely not...

"Is that a… a… a REINDEER?"

3

ELF RESPECT

"Well, of course it's a reindeer. What else would it be?" The voice was still talking to me from behind the hedge but that wasn't where I was looking. "Of course, it's not just any old reindeer. This is Gladys. She is the happiest of all Santa's reindeer and can always be relied upon to cheer you up, no matter how sad you are. Happiness is even in her name – 'GLADys'. That's why I brought her with me, as I definitely need cheering up.

All thanks to you."

I'd barely noticed that he'd stopped talking as I just couldn't stop watching Gladys. She was both magnificent and absolutely mesmerising.

"You do know it's rude to stare?"

I could feel my tongue and teeth getting cold and slowly realised it was because my mouth was hanging open. I quickly closed it. I also realised that the voice was quite correct; I was staring and I did know that it was rude. Not that I could tell him, for my attention was quite firmly fixed upon the huge reindeer that had its head hanging over the hedge. It also seemed to be smiling.

I didn't even know that reindeer could smile!

"Excuse me? Hello?" The voice was talking to me but I was still desperately trying to stop watching Gladys. That was definitely her name. She had a chain with a string of bells that hung around her neck with a small and shiny brass plaque that had *'Gladys'* in bright red letters that seemed to sparkle as it swayed. Of course, I was definitely *not* staring, because that would be quite rude. In the midst of my watching, I felt a tug at my trousers, just below my knee. It was only after I was tugged for a second time did I manage to drag my eyes away from Gladys long enough to look down to see what was demanding my attention.

My mouth immediately fell open.

Again.

"Ah, I have your attention now, do I? Don't tell me you're going to start staring at me now. I hope not. That would also be very rude. Santa marks staring on his Naughty List, just so you know. Although you running away from home, and upsetting your mum, has you very high on his Naughty List already."

"Are you an… an…?" I really couldn't bring myself to ask as I was afraid that this

might also be considered rude. There was no point upsetting Santa any further.

Or my mum.

Yet I also couldn't quite believe what I was seeing.

"An elf? Is that what you are asking? Am I an elf?" The voice came from a head that barely reached my knee. I have never seen anyone this small before in my life, that's almost a full ten years. A very long time indeed. As he asked me the question, all I could do was nod my head, yet my mouth was still open. So as I nodded, my teeth banged together as my head went up and down.

I must have looked so silly.

"Well of course I'm an elf. What did you expect? However, I am not just any old elf. I am *your* elf. That's why I am here." He stabbed his finger into my knee as he pointed up at me. It was quite sore, but I didn't let him see that he hurt me at all. I was, after all, a brave boy.

"My elf? What do you mean, you are my elf? I didn't even know that I had an elf."

Really, I didn't.

"Everybody has an elf. Mrs. Claus makes sure of that. She allocates every single child – all over the world – their very own elf, right at the very minute they are born. We are responsible for watching you throughout the year to see if you have been naughty or nice, and reporting directly back to her. Then she and Santa decide what gifts you will receive from your list, based on how naughty or nice you've been. That's when we get to work, making all your presents and wrapping them up, all ready for Santa to deliver on Christmas Eve."

As the elf was telling me this, he'd stopped poking me with his little finger and had started feeding a carrot to Gladys. She ate it quicker than I have ever seen anybody eating anything, and then gently nudged him with her huge head. He turned his back to me and whispered very softly into the ear of the massive reindeer, trying to ensure I couldn't hear him.

But I could.

"Now Gladys, don't be greedy. You know that I can only give you just the one carrot. Santa has very strict instructions. Any more than this makes you… well, you know…?"

Gladys looked at me and seemed totally confused. Me too. The elf looked at her, then at me, then turned back to her. He buried his head back down into her ear and covered his mouth as he tried to whisper even more quietly than before. Once again, I heard every single word.

"You know fine well that they make you fart!"

Gladys winked at me then she proudly lifted her head as high as it would go. She seemed to have an even bigger smile than before, if that was even possible. I used both my hands to cover my face and even bit my cheeks to stop myself from laughing, but I simply couldn't.

"What's so funny?" The elf was serious. Maybe even angry, I really couldn't tell.

"*Well, it's just... hahaha... well, carrots... hahaha... carrots... hahaha... they... hahaha... well they make me fart too!*" I was really struggling to breathe, far less speak, from laughing. A few minutes later, when I eventually did manage to compose myself, I could see he was not happy.

Not happy at all.

"So, what's your name?" I thought it best to at least try and be friendly. It would definitely be rude to simply call him 'elf'. Even if it wasn't, I couldn't risk it. Suddenly I very much wanted to be off the Naughty and back on the Nice List.

"Oh, that's an easy one, but you should already know the answer." The elf was now pouring some milk into a saucer and laid it on the ground in front of Gladys. It seems she can drink as quickly as she can eat. If not even quicker. I really wanted some milk too but didn't want to ask.

"I should? How? I mean, why should I already know the answer?" This was very confusing.

"Every elf is given the exact same name as the child that they are allocated to watch. So my name is the same as yours. Although, I wish I could say that it is very nice to meet you, Gabriel."

Both he and Gladys were looking directly at me.

"But it's not."

4

ELF CONTROL

"Why is it not nice to meet me? What have I ever done to you?" I could feel the tears swelling heavily in my eyes but I was determined not to cry. Big boys – brave boys – don't cry.

Ever.

That's a fact. Everybody knows that.

"It's not nice to meet you because you say you don't believe in Santa Claus. Do you know what happens to me when you stop believing in Santa Claus? No? I didn't think so! That's why we are here, to tell you exactly what happens." Gabriel the Elf had his hands firmly on his hips and his head was tilted to the side. His mouth was all crumpled up and looked like my gran's does when she wants to give me a kiss, although I could tell that he certainly didn't want to do that – thankfully. On either side of his slim nose, he'd scrunched up his tiny eyes until they were almost completely hidden underneath even tinier eyebrows. It was almost funny, but I already knew better than to say that to him. He was trying really hard to look angry – he was definitely not happy – and I immediately wondered what his face would look like with a smile. Certainly different, maybe even pleasant. Between his two pointy ears there was a green hat with a red pom-pom that looked as if it would fall off his head at any moment.

I was ready to catch it if it did.

"You see, Santa…" As he started speaking, he seemed completely unaware of the new set of headlights coming towards us. Only, this time, they were heading back towards the town from the village. The snow had briefly stopped but was now falling heavy again and causing the car to go even slower than before.

"I'm sorry, and I truly don't mean to be rude, but I really must hide. You see, if that car sees me, then they will tell my mum and I'll be in even more trouble." As I pointed towards the car's headlights, Gabriel the Elf completely ignored me.

"…and don't get me started on poor old Doris. She was banished after only five years. She never, ever, came back because big Doris grew up and never had any children of her own. Well, that meant she never grew up to really believe in Santa Claus again. Poor old Doris…"

The car was making its way slowly through the snow and around the last of the bends, and then it would definitely see us. How could it not? We were the only people here and we were stood right beside the road. Gladys was happily resting her head on top of the hedge, staring at Gabriel the Elf and seeming to understand every word he was saying.

I wanted to ask if her staring was rude, but I was far too concerned with the car.

There was no other option, we all had to hide. If the car saw Gabriel the Elf and Gladys, then they would have to explain why they were here – I certainly couldn't. Then whoever was in the car would just take me home. Back to my mum. They would definitely not take me to my dad and that's exactly where I wanted to go. No, there was definitely no other choice, we all had to hide. As I went to move back into the gap in the hedge, Gabriel the Elf stepped in front of it and blocked me. Gladys had moved slowly behind the hedge and I could now see her long legs through the gap.

Gabriel the Elf was still talking.

"I'm sorry, but can you please move? We need to hide!" I tried to move around him and into the safety of the scary forest.

"So you see, it was the story of old Doris that brought me here. You understand that, don't you? I just had to come. I don't want to be banished and never heard from again. All my friends live at the North Pole and I love it there. We have so much fun, watching all you children, and Santa and Mrs. Claus are just the best. Ask anyone! Aren't they just the best Gladys?"

I thought my eyes must be going wonky as I'm sure I saw Gladys nod in agreement as she looked at Gabriel the Elf and then back at me. I didn't have time to ask if she understood. *"PLEASE!* Can't you see the car? I have to hide. If they see me, they will take me back to my mum and I want to go to my dad."

"What's wrong with going back to your mum?" Gabriel the Elf looked me straight in the eye as he asked the question. Almost staring at me. He seemed really concerned and wanted to know. Nobody ever listens to me so why would he care? It didn't really matter as there was no time to tell him. I was about to be caught and taken back home anyway.

The car had come around the very last bend and now had us in its headlights. I closed my eyes in the hope that it wouldn't see me. I could hear the engine getting closer and closer. Any second now, it would completely slow down and stop.

"She's a lovely woman, your mum. Her elf is also lovely, well-matched those two…" He was still talking and totally ignoring me.

As I heard the car get closer and closer, I closed my eyes tighter and tighter. Then the strangest thing ever happened. Well, the second strangest thing ever. The strangest thing ever happened only a little while ago when I met both Gabriel the Elf and Gladys the Reindeer.

The second strangest thing that ever happened was when the car drove right passed us.

"Well? You still haven't told what's wrong with going back to your lovely mum?" I hadn't noticed that he had been quiet and impatiently waiting for my answer. He seemed to be rather cross although I had no idea why.

After all, she was my mum, not his.

"The car, why didn't it stop?" The taillights disappeared around another bend on the way back to town.

"Why would it stop? They can't see us. Only very special people are allowed to see us. Now you, being in the shadow of Gladys and myself, well that means that nobody can see you either. So, are you ever going to tell me what's wrong with you and your mum? You see, us elves, we know that it's good to talk. *'A problem shared is a problem halved'* that's what Santa always says. Isn't that right Gladys?" Again Gladys just nodded as she looked between Gabriel the Elf and myself. "If you share your problem enough, and it gets halved so many times, then it's no longer a problem. Do you see?"

"It doesn't matter. You won't understand." He really wouldn't. How could he? Living at the North Pole with Santa and Mrs. Claus, all the other elves, and with all the reindeer. It's nothing like living in my village. Or in the town.

"Of course, I *don't* understand. That doesn't mean that I *won't* understand. There is a big difference and that is, after all, why I'm here to see you!" Gladys had been looking at me and happily nodding with everything that Gabriel the Elf had been saying. Yet, when he stopped talking this time, Gladys suddenly looked a little cross. She turned and bit the elf's pom-pom and took it clean off his head.

"Hey! What are you doing? Give that back to…" Gabriel the Elf was jumping as high as he could, trying to reach for his hat when he saw the look on Gladys' face. It was

then that he understood why she had taken it.

"I'm sorry, Gladys. I should have said that is why WE are here to see you! Are you happy now? Can I please have my hat back?" Gladys gave another huge smile as she dropped the hat and, leaning over to me, gave me a big sticky lick on my cheek.

5

THE SNOW GLOBE

"Christmas is rubbish. Every year I get rubbish presents and it's always because we have no money. Some of the other kids at school tell me we are poor. I don't think we're poor, but then I'm not really sure what being poor really means. I thought it meant we have no money but, when I asked my mum, she said that's not what being poor is at all. Of course, she also told me that I was the richest little boy in the world, and I know that isn't true. So now I really don't know what to believe." It was only when I stopped talking did I realise that I had sat down on the ground.

In the snow.

My bottom was freezing.

Gabriel the Elf and Gladys the Reindeer were both staring at me and not saying a single word; they'd just let me talk. Now that I'd finished, there was silence. A really awkward silence. They seemed to be waiting for me to say more, but I had nothing more to say.

"So this is your problem? That your mum has no money and your dad does? So if you go and live with your dad then your problem will be solved?" Gabriel the Elf had been right, he could – and, more importantly, did – understand. This made me instantly happy. Maybe he was right, sharing my problem with him and Gladys had now split my problem into three pieces.

I now only had one-third of a problem and it did feel so much better.

"Exactly. I'm so glad that you understand. I didn't know if you would. Oh how I wish my mum was as understanding as you!"

"You should know that there is a big difference between understanding and agreeing. This is one of those times. I understand what you think is your problem, but I certainly don't agree with you; especially when your mum is correct. You most definitely are the richest little boy in the world. You are also one of the luckiest. I think it's time we showed you why. What do you think Gladys?" Gabriel the Elf turned to the huge reindeer whose massive smile seemed to get even bigger and brighter with every word. She was now nodding very excitedly at the suggestion from the tiny elf.

"Look here." Gabriel the Elf held a snow globe in his hand. Although not exactly in his hand, it was more floating ever so slightly above it. *Where did he get that?* It really was too large for him to have been carrying in his pockets – I wasn't even sure if he had

any pockets. If he did, then I would definitely have noticed something so obvious, and yet I never saw anything. I quickly looked at Gladys, but immediately realised that she didn't have any hands so would have no use for pockets.

Where did it come from?

"What are you looking for? Have you lost something? You're supposed to be looking into here…" He pointed then tapped at the snow globe "…not everywhere else. You don't need to know where it came from. That's part of the magic."

It's like he could read my mind.

"I'm sorry." I really was, but I wasn't sure why. It was either because he had caught me looking around or because he had caught me not looking into the snow globe. Maybe both. Either way, I was sorry. I also felt rather silly that he had caught me at all and, strangely, that he knew what I was searching for.

Maybe he actually did just read my mind.

I quickly decided that it was better to just do as he told me and so I looked straight into the snow globe. Although I couldn't help but wonder how it was able to just float in the air like that. Maybe he really could perform magic. Just as this thought came to me, I saw my dad and his new family in their living room.

All inside the snow globe!

"What is this? What's happening?" I was very confused.

"You think everything will be better at your dad's new house, so I thought we would go and see." Gabriel the Elf was staring at me – *how rude* – but I didn't care. I was completely fascinated by what I was seeing inside the snow globe.

"Go and see? What do you mean 'go and see'?" I was becoming even more confused.

You need to look inside – really look inside." Gabriel the Elf was using his other hand and pointing into the very centre of the snow globe. As I bent forward to get a better look, something very strange happened.

Very strange indeed.

Suddenly we were pulled inside the snow globe and were now standing in my dad's living room.

6

FATHER'S CHRISTMAS

"Is that your dad? It looks like he is getting ready to leave for work." Gabriel the Elf was right. My dad was very smartly dressed in a uniform with a shiny hat. It wasn't a cool hat with a pom-pom, and certainly nowhere near as colourful, but his had a badge and only special people have them.

Like sheriffs and policemen.

"He works in a bank. My mum told me that he has a very important job there. He protects people's money and keeps it safe from all the bandits, thieves, and highwaymen. I don't really know what bandits and highwaymen are, but thieves steal things and he stops them. He must be very important if he needs to work on Christmas Day."

It made me very happy to see that Gladys was nodding in agreement. Gabriel the Elf wasn't paying any attention to what I was saying. Instead, he was looking at the two children in the living room. They were both older than me and their mum was my dad's new wife.

They were all my dad's new family.

"So you want to live here – away from your mum – and with them? That seems rather odd to me, if you don't mind me saying. It doesn't look like much fun, does it?" Gladys was shaking her head, but still seeming to agree. I thought that you only nodded your head when you agree? Maybe I was wrong, but not as wrong as Gladys the Reindeer or Gabriel the Elf. They were so wrong. So very, very wrong. Living here would be brilliant fun!

"What are you talking about? Can't you see what they have? Can you not see what they're doing?" I certainly could and it was amazing. "The girl is playing with her brand new cell phone. I mean, it's a brand new cell phone! Mum won't allow me to have a one as it *'kills the art of conversation'* according to her. Whatever that means? Look at the boy, he has a brand new tablet computer! Can you not see the empty box behind his seat? Their mum is watching the biggest television that I think I have ever seen. This would be the best house ever to live in!"

Gabriel the Elf looked at the boy, then the girl, then at their mum, then at Gladys. They both started shaking their heads as he finally turned to look at me.

"I must be missing something. All I see is your dad saying goodbye to his new family so that he can go off to work on Christmas Day. I mean, who works on

Christmas Day? Even so, everyone is ignoring him. Every single one of them." Gladys was nodding again. I'm guessing she was agreeing because everything Gabriel the Elf had just said was absolutely true. Dad was standing at the living room door with a small bag in his hand and saying goodbye, and yet nobody paid him any attention.

Except me.

I knew he couldn't see me but, just in case he could, I turned my back slightly to hide my hand from Gabriel the Elf and Gladys, and gave him a little wave. Out of the corner of my mouth I whispered, "Hi Dad, Merry Christmas." I was right, he couldn't see me. He disappeared behind the living room door, closing it behind him, and out of the house. I watched him through the window as he trudged through the snow and away into the distance.

Nobody else in the living room seemed to know, or care, that he was gone.

"So, if you lived here now, your dad would be gone and you would be doing what? Playing on your own with a cell phone or a computer? That doesn't sound like much fun to me. Gladys and I, in fact everyone that lives at the North Pole with Santa, is encouraged to play and talk and have fun. For most of the year that's what we do, all day, every day!"

Gladys gave Gabriel the Elf another big lick. I really wouldn't have minded if she had given me one too.

"You don't understand. Cell phones and tablet computers are just awesome!" As I

watched the boy and the girl playing with theirs, I was thinking about what Gabriel the Elf had just said. I didn't really believe what I was saying, but I couldn't tell him or Gladys that though. That would be to admit I was wrong and I really wasn't. Cell phones and laptops are awesome!

Maybe just not as awesome as I first thought.

"Gladys, do you think that this is maybe what happens to the banished elves? They have to play with cell phones and laptops all day at the South Pole?" Gabriel the Elf seemed very concerned by the thought.

Once again, Gladys was nodding in agreement but, this time, she looked rather sad.

"The South Pole? What do you mean the South Pole?" Everyone knows that Santa and his elves and the reindeer all live at the North Pole, not the South Pole, don't they? It was my turn to be concerned. I was also confused.

Again.

"Well that's what happens to the elves when their child stops believing in Santa Claus, they are banished to the South Pole until the child believes in Santa again. Sometimes, this is very quick, and they are only gone for a very short time. Other times, they are never seen again. The elves that have come back tell us that it's not very much fun at the South Pole and they far prefer being in the North Pole. They aren't allowed to tell us anything else about their time there or they could be sent back. However, now that I have seen what happens with cell phones and laptops, I can only imagine that they have lots and lots of them at the South Pole."

"If that's true, then I wish I lived in the South Pole." It must be absolutely fantastic there, although I did say this out loud without really thinking.

"Don't you ever say that! It's a horrible place, all the elves that have ever come back from there say so. Nobody talks with each other or plays together. I don't ever want to go there, that's why I am here. To assure you that Santa is very real. And so am I." As he finished talking, Gladys once again bit his hat and took it off his head. Only, this time, she shook it so hard that all of the bells around her neck began to chime. It was a nice sound, I really liked it. It sounded like Jingle Bells but I couldn't be absolutely sure. What was certain was the drool that she left on the hat – it seemed to be soaked through!

"Ok, ok, I'm sorry. Of course, you are very real too. Now, can I have my hat back please?" Gladys dropped the hat and Gabriel the Elf had to take a second to wring it out. There was a whole lot of drool in his hat and I tried really hard not to laugh, but I couldn't help myself. It was just too funny. When I looked up at Gladys she winked at me and smiled.

"So you think that having lots of money to buy lots of toys and other things would make you happy? That you would then have no worries at all?" Gabriel the Elf was asking me the questions, but I really couldn't talk, so I just nodded. His hat was hanging down over his face and there was some of Gladys' drool just hanging from the end of the red pom-pom. He obviously didn't know about it, or he just didn't care. It was still funny to me and if I tried to answer him, I'm sure I would have started to laugh again.

Now I know how really rude that would be.

"Ok, well let's just see if you're right." Once again, as if by magic, he suddenly had the snow globe in his hand. I really had no idea where it came from. As I was looking all around trying to figure it out, he clicked his fingers to draw my attention back to him.

"Just look in here…"

7

ELF ASSURED

"Where is this place?"

Once again we had all been pulled back inside the snow globe and were now in a totally new room. There were pictures on every wall, but they were nothing like the pictures in our house. Those were mostly pictures of me when I was much younger, like seven or eight. Mum hasn't put up any recent pictures of me all grown up, now that I'm so very nearly ten. No, these pictures were of really old people who looked very important. The walls were strange and didn't have any colourful wallpaper, but were all brown and made of wood.

Yet that's not what I first saw.

There, sitting at the window and looking outside at the snow, was a little girl. I've never seen a seat like hers. It looked more like a throne or, at least, what I think a throne

would look like. Whatever kind of seat it was, I really liked it. It would be a great place to sit with all my friends and pretend that I was the king. Well, maybe just a prince. Kings are a lot older than me. It would be just perfect if there was a table in the middle where we could all play cards and board games. My friends wouldn't have thrones though; they would have just normal seats. We would never need to move as we could eat at that table too.

That would be just awesome.

"Do you know why the little girl is crying?" I turned to see Gabriel the Elf looking straight at her. It was only then did I see the big tears in his eyes. Gladys too. I hadn't even noticed she was crying. Now that I did, it made me sad too.

"No, why is she crying?" I really wanted to know as there was absolutely no reason for her to cry. Not that I could see anyway. Hers was easily the best playroom in the world!

"Don't you see the unopened presents under the tree?" Gabriel the Elf was still watching her as he pointed towards another corner of the room, directly opposite the little girl, and on the other side of the fireplace. The fire was beautiful, really big and bright, and I didn't really see the tree at first because of all the gifts. They weren't really under the tree, but rather they seemed to be everywhere. They were built all up and around it, even hanging from every branch. At the very top could I see the Christmas fairy nearly touching the ceiling – she must have been terrified.

"Why doesn't she open her presents? They look amazing!" They really did and I wouldn't know where to start with opening them all.

"She doesn't want the presents." Gabriel the Elf seemed to know what she was thinking, although I have no idea how. Maybe he could read her mind too.

"What? Why? That's crazy!" Who wouldn't want all these brilliant presents? Even if they were to be wasted on a girl.

"She has nobody to share them with and she is looking out the window, waiting for her parents."

"Waiting for her parents? Is that not her mum sitting right there?" I helpfully pointed to the lady who was sitting quietly on the other side of the fireplace, next to all the presents and the tree.

"No, that's not her mum. That's her nanny. That is the person that looks after her instead of her mum and dad. Her parents have gone out skiing but have promised to come back to see her open her presents. She was still asleep when they left this morning, so now she must wait for them to return before she is allowed to open them. The nanny will be fired if she lets her open even one while they are gone." As he finished speaking, Gabriel the Elf took off his own hat and blew his nose into it. He turned to Gladys and held it up for her and she blew her nose into it too. Then he just placed it back on his head, throwing his pom-pom behind one of his pointy ears.

At that very moment, I really wanted one of those hats. Instead, I had to just settle for wiping my eyes and nose on my sleeve. It was only then that I noticed that I'd also been crying, although it wasn't really crying. Not really. I was just sad and my eyes leaked a little. My nose too. It was only when I'd finished did I see that they'd been watching me. Both of them. They then looked at each other and started shaking their heads.

"What?" I asked the question, but didn't know if it was rude or not.

"That's disgusting. You really need a hat." Gladys the Reindeer was nodding enthusiastically in complete agreement with Gabriel the Elf.

"Well, I don't have one. I only have my sleeve, so that will have to do." I was just glad they hadn't thought I was crying. After all, that isn't what big boys do, is it? "So this little girl must just sit here and wait for her mum and dad after having already waited for ages on Santa?" It seemed like Santa was everywhere I looked for as long as I could remember – on every television, on every radio, in every store.

Absolutely everywhere.

"Yes, but it looks like her wait is finally over." Gabriel the Elf pointed towards the door that was slowly opening into the living room. It probably wasn't that slowly, but it just seemed that way to me. Really slow.

Much like waiting for Christmas…and for Santa!

I guessed it was her parents as it was a man and a woman that came into the room. They didn't seem very happy and I could hear the man whisper, 'We shouldn't have bought Christina so many presents. It will take such a long time for her to open them all.' The woman whispered back, 'Yes I know, but it is Christmas, darling. This will only take a few minutes, then we can get back to having our holiday. She goes back to boarding school in a few days, so not too long.'

Their whispers weren't very quiet.

"Is the little girl's name Christina? Surely they aren't talking about her?" My mum would never talk about me like this. She would never want to get rid of me so she could have fun without me.

Never ever.

"I'm afraid so. What's worse is that they think that Christina doesn't know, but she does. She is like you, very clever." I didn't want to ask how he knew I was clever. Actually, he said I was 'very clever'. Whether I was clever or very clever, it didn't really matter, it was the nicest thing anyone has ever said to me.

Except, of course, for my mum.

"I think we should go as we don't have the time to wait for Christina to open all of her presents. She doesn't know we are here so our leaving won't upset her any more than she already is. By the looks of things, it is going to take even longer than her mum thinks." Gabriel the Elf drew my attention away from her parents and back to the little girl.

She hadn't moved.

"But her parents are here now, so why isn't she rushing to open all of her presents?" If it was me, as soon as they'd opened the door, I'd have run straight into the middle of the mountain of presents that surrounded the Christmas tree and started tearing away at anything that my hands touched.

"As I said, you are very clever. Take a second and think about it." Gabriel the Elf took off his hat again and felt that it was still soaked with a mixture of both his and Gladys the Reindeer's tears and drool. He placed it back on his head and turned his back to me, thinking I couldn't see – but I did.

He had wiped his nose with his sleeve.

I didn't say anything but it did make me smile. As I was thinking about Christina, I felt something on my own sleeve. It was Gladys…wiping her nose!

"She doesn't want the presents. She just wants the time with her parents!" As I said it, I realised that Gabriel the Elf was right. I was clever.

Very clever.

"Correct. That is all she wants for Christmas, simply to spend this time with her family. So now do you understand? You don't need money to be rich." Once again, Gabriel the Elf held the snow globe in his hand. *Where does he get it from?* This time, however, I knew exactly what to do.

As it began to hover ever so slightly above his hand, I looked straight into it.

8

HOME ALONE

"You must have made a mistake. This is my home. Why would you bring me here?" It had only been a short time ago that I'd ran away from this house and it just looked the same. Nothing had changed. A weak fire looked even smaller in the large fireplace. Our sparsely decorated Christmas tree seemed even more pathetic when I compared it to Christina's, and ours only had a few presents underneath – although every one of them was for me.

I hadn't noticed before that there wasn't a single present for my mum.

"Oh there is no mistake. None at all. Just wait a minute, there is something you need to see." Gabriel the Elf was watching the door intently. So was Gladys. After a few seconds, my mum came through from the kitchen with a cup of tea.

It looked like she had been crying.

"Why does she look so sad?" My eyes were suddenly stinging from the tears that had instantly appeared and were now rolling down my cheeks.

"Mum…! Mum…!"

"She can't hear you. She can't see you either. As long as you are with us, nobody can see or hear you. Well, except us of course. Don't you remember?" Gabriel the Elf's voice was now very soft and quiet as Gladys gently rested her head on his shoulder. It seemed to me that she was giving the little elf a hug. Gabriel the Elf simply raised his arm up and wrapped it around Gladys's massive head.

Could nobody see that I really needed a hug too?

"Anyway, what do you care? This is how your mum is going to be spending her Christmas when you go and live with your dad and his new family."

"I never knew my mum would be so sad about me going." I truly didn't. But then, I'd never really thought about it.

"Of course, she would be sad. You're all she has. She doesn't even have a present under the tree, and she doesn't want nor need one. Do you know what I have here?" Gabriel the Elf dug deep into his pocket and pulled out a little piece of paper.

"No, what is it?" It was too small to be anything important.

"It's your mum's Christmas Wish List for Santa. Here, read what it says." He handed me the piece of paper. She only asked for one thing.

Dear Santa
All I want is for my son Gabriel
to be the happiest
little boy in the world.
Thank you

Dear Santa,

All I want is for my son Gabriel to be the happiest little boy in the world.

Thank you.

"She didn't ask for anything for herself, only for me. Why would she do that?" I really didn't understand and was very confused.

"Oh that's easy. She only wants you to be happy because she is your mum!" Gladys seemed to understand what Gabriel the Elf meant as she gave him another big lick on his face. Then she gave me one too.

It was the best lick I've ever had.

"I think there is one last place you need to see. All you need to do is have another look inside my snow globe…"

9

HOMEWARD BOUND

"Gabriel…? Gabriel…? Are you awake? Santa's been and left you lots of presents!"

"Mum? Is that you? Can you see me?" I quickly opened my eyes and saw that I was in bed. My own bed. At home. My back was to my mum and I was facing the wall. Like always.

"Of course, I can see you, silly goose! Are you coming down to open your presents? They won't open themselves, you know." My mum sounded so excited. "Are Gabriel the Elf and Gladys the Reindeer still here? Can you see them?" I didn't want to move in the hope that they were still here with me, but I just knew that they weren't.

"Gabriel the Elf and Gladys the Reindeer? No, they aren't here. It's just you and me, I'm afraid. It sounds like you had the best dream though. Or maybe you met them

when Santa was here to drop off your presents?" I knew from Mum's voice that she didn't believe me, but I liked that she pretended that she did. "Speaking of which, are you coming downstairs to open them? I really want to know what Santa brought you. If you don't come quickly, I may have to start opening them on my own." With that, Mum turned and closed the door and I heard her making her way downstairs.

I knew she would never really open my presents, but, still, I couldn't risk it. I jumped out of bed and raced downstairs and managed to pass her in the hallway before she made it to the living room door. It was only then that I saw that she had the most brilliant smile I've ever seen, even bigger and better than Gladys the Reindeer's!

When I entered the living room, everything looked different. The Christmas tree was bigger and brighter than I remembered. The fire was roaring and filled up the whole hearth. Then there were the presents under the tree – there were so many. Far more than I ever imagined.

"Santa really has been, hasn't he, Mum?"

"Yes, he really has. He drank some of his milk that we left for him, and he ate all the cookies. The reindeer – sorry, Gladys as you called her – even had some of the carrot." As I looked at the table, I couldn't believe my eyes!

"Mum, is that drool on the end of the carrot?" It was shining in the firelight and almost dripping off the table.

"Why yes, I think it is." She was smiling at me, but I knew it was real. "So, what present shall you open first?"

I looked under the tree and picked up the present at the very top of the pile. It was perfectly wrapped in paper of such bright and wonderful colours, and all tied up in a bright red bow. As I pulled the ribbon, all the wrapping paper just fell away. There in my hand, was a...

"What is that?" Mum asked the question as if she had never ever seen this before. "It's absolutely beautiful."

"It's a snow globe." It was then that I knew exactly what to do. "It seems that this had my name on it by mistake. This is a present for you, Mum."

As I handed it to her, she started to cry. "Are you sure this is for me?" She was holding the snow globe in her hand when I suddenly saw movement inside it. There, I could clearly see Gabriel the Elf and Gladys the Reindeer at the North Pole. They were standing outside the front of a house with a big snowman in the garden. Gabriel the Elf was pointing to the house and then back to himself.

Ah, this is your home!

It was then that I knew that they would always be close with me, living right there inside the snow globe. Never again would I doubt the existence of Santa. Gladys gave him another big lick and Gabriel the Elf once again took off his hat and used it to wipe her drool from his face. He put it back on his head and threw the pom-pom behind one of his big pointy ears. Then his face suddenly filled the whole snow globe and he gave me a wink and a huge smile, and then they were gone.

All that was left inside the snow globe was the house and the snowman.

"I really don't think this is for me. Are you sure?" Mum was as happy as I have ever seen her. She was looking so deeply into the snow globe that I thought for a second that she might suddenly disappear. Then I realised that was just silly.

Or was it?

"I am absolutely certain that it's for you. It's the most perfect present I could ever give to the most perfect mum ever. Merry Christmas." She didn't say a single word as she reached around and gave me the biggest and tightest hug that made me feel all tingly inside.

"You are the best little boy any mum could ever wish for. I love you, my darling." She kissed the top of my head and I squeezed as hard as I could around her waist...

"I love you too, Mum."

GABRIEL THE ELF

Gabriel the Elf would like to invite you to visit his website for updates from the North Pole and details of his most recent adventures.

www.gabrieltheelf.com

ABOUT THE AUTHOR

After graduating with a couple of useless degrees in law, Alexander McCabe left his native Scotland and wandered nomadically around the globe to experience the rich diversity of culture that the world has to offer. Along the way, he met his wonderful wife. Together, they have one son. His name is a closely held family secret.

Oh wait...

Connect with Alexander McCabe

www.aasmccabe.com